Storytime
for Grown-Up Women

and the girls who will become them

Deborah Monk

Hudson, NH

Storytime for Grown-up Women
and the girls who will become them
by
Deborah Monk

ISBN: 978-1-7323384-2-5

Cover Design & Interior Design:
Pamela Marin-Kingsley:
pammarin-kingsley.com & chromatostudio.com

Published by:
LifePondering Press
Hudson, New Hampshire
website: deborahmonk.com
Contact: deb@deborahmonk.com

Table of Contents

Be Good. Be Quiet. Behave.
Imagine, instead, if
we taught our girls to be brave.

Wings and a Tail

When I was little, I had fairy wings and a mermaid tail.

Sometimes, when I tried to run really fast, I would trip over my tail. So one day I asked, “Mama, can you cut off my tail?”

“If I cut off your tail,” she said, “you won’t be able to dive under the bubbles in your bath. You won’t be able to find the treasure chest where you keep your dreams.”

“That’s ok, Mama,” I said, “because running really fast with my friends is one of my dreams.”

"Part of growing up is fitting in," Mama said. "But you have to be careful not to give away too much of your magic."

"If you cut off my tail, can it grow back?" I asked.

"It will if you remember you had it."

I nodded, so Mama got scissors and cut off my tail. She saved a tiny piece and carefully wrapped it in tissue paper.

"Don't forget," she whispered. "You are a brave mermaid who can dive deep to find life's treasures."

"I won't forget, Mama," I promised.

A couple years later in ballet class, I noticed that my friends could turn more times because they didn't have wings slowing them down.

"Mama, can you cut off my wings?"

"You already cut off your tail," she said. "Are you sure you want to cut off your wings, too?"

"You said they will grow back whenever I want. I just have to remember that I had them."

"Yes, I did, darling. But it's so easy to forget."

"I won't forget," I promised as she cut off my wings.

Then I got very busy growing up; fitting in and doing all the things everyone expected. I was happy. . . but I was also forgetting.

One day after work, I called home. "I got a promotion," I told Mama.

"Congratulations," she said.

We were both quiet for a moment.

"How come you're not happy?" she asked.

"Because while my boss was giving me the promotion, he said I have to work harder." I sighed. "I'm already working so hard."

"What are you going to do?" Mama asked.

"I guess I'll just have to work harder."

"You could look in your heart," she whispered.

"That's your answer to everything," I grumbled.

"Have you tried it?" she asked.

"I've been too busy working, getting ahead, and doing everything I'm supposed to be doing."

"Do you remember when you believed you were a mermaid who had a hidden treasure chest of dreams?" she asked.

"Mama, I live in a big city. There is no place to dive to find hidden treasure."

"Remember when you had wings that let you fly above any words people might say to you that weren't nice?"

"What good are wings," I asked, "if everyone I love is anchored to the ground?"

The next morning I woke up and sat on the edge of my bed. I didn't want to get dressed in my itchy business suit. And I had no desire to go to work where they didn't think I was good enough.

"Look in your heart," Mama's voice whispered in my head.

I took a deep breath and put my hand over my heart. I felt something I had never noticed before. A little bump. A seam. The edge of a pocket.

Inside my heart pocket I found two pieces of tissue paper. I carefully unwrapped one and found a piece of a beautiful wing. I closed my eyes and remembered. When I opened my eyes, the piece had disappeared from my hand. I looked in the mirror.

My wings were back, bigger than before. For a moment I was embarrassed. What would people at work say if I showed up with wings?

I unwrapped the second tissue paper from my heart pocket and found a tiny piece of my mermaid tail. I closed my eyes.

Again, I remembered.

When I opened my eyes, I saw my tail, graceful and fluid, floating behind me.

I loved having my wings and tail back, but I was scared. Since the pieces had disappeared, I had nothing left to remind me.

I was afraid if I gave my wings and tail up again, I might never get them back.

Taking the tip of one wing, I draped it over my shoulder like a glamorous shawl. Then I bustled my tail like a hip scarf and tied it around my waist.

Now I have wings to fly above everything that is not suited for my soul. . . and a mermaid tail because I want to swim in the deep end of life.

I learned that part of growing up is reclaiming my wings and a tail.

The
Dancing
Acorn

Once upon a time, I was an acorn.
Frolicking on the winds of adventure,
I touched down only long enough
to taste delicious freedom.
With fields of golden dreams
blossoming in my heart,
I embodied the dance of exploration.

When the sands of time
started humming a new tune,
I planted roots deep into the earth
to keep me steady and strong.
I held hands with Mother Nature
and swayed to the dance of grounding.

Branches, my open arms, cradled our nest.
Leaves of orange and red,
an umbrella of burgeoning colors,
sheltered my loved ones.
The wind, a soft inhale and exhale,
our lullaby.

Seasons came and went without time.
I watched everyone else grow,
evolve, and change form.
My baby became a toddler.
A child. A girl.
An acorn now, she prances away
on the wings of her own adventure.

I am nothing but a tree.
A tree is a tree is a tree.
Branches sagging.
Leaves falling.
Stripped of color.
An observer of change,
waiting for nothing.

Then Mother Nature tickles my roots
with a question.
"Who do you want to be
when you grow up?"
I answer simply.
"An acorn is to become a tree."
An elm of a daughter.
A willow of a wife.
An oak of a mother.

"We ask the acorn,
what do you want to be
when you grow up," she responds.
"But we ask the tree. . .
who do you want to be?"

"I want to be the tree that is most me,"
I whisper,
wondering. . .
when did being me
become the hardest thing to be?

The earth quivers.
Internal contractions.
A birth of myself.
Lyrics of a soul song,
almost forgotten,
take me back in time.
"Begin. . . again. Become. . . again.

The wisdom of women warriors
thunders through my blood and
I harness the light
of a thousand shooting stars.
As my soul plants fully in my body,
I dance with the knowledge…
I am bursting with potential!

The
Lost Lamb

Once upon a time, I was frolicking through life on the Good Girl Trail. The herd was my home, my family, my world. For a long while, everything was fine.

Until it wasn't.

Dad died, friends wandered off, and Mom disappeared around the bend in the moon.

Suddenly, I was alone with no one to lead the way.

Lost within, and lost without, could I be more lost than lost in myself?

I kept moving forward and came to a fork. To my left, the Stay Safe Trail was busy and bright. To my right, the Stay True Trail was deserted and dim.

My legs trembled—the choice should have been simple. I wanted to chase dreams and stop chasing my tail.

But simple didn't mean easy and I was afraid to move. I closed my eyes, wishing for courage, and when I opened them, I saw a shoe store tucked in the woods, just out of sight.

Wanting answers but hearing only questions, I went into the store to ask for directions.

"I can't tell you which way to go," the clerk said with a smile. "That is something only you can know."

I *wanted* to be true but I *needed* to feel safe. I sighed. "Maybe I should just follow the herd, where *Go Along to Get Along* is the favorite song."

The clerk nodded. "It is an easier trail, and you'll have plenty of company. But the price of taking the Stay Safe Trail is high. The music of the herd will drown out your own heart song."

I stood up straight and my heart skipped a beat. "I have a heart song?" I asked in a hopeful whisper. "Why haven't I heard it?"

"Not to worry," he said. "It's always there, even when you aren't listening." He led me over to the shelves on the wall. "Whichever trail you choose, you'll need the right shoes. Take your time and find what suits you."

I spied the bunny slippers, all comfy and soft. No self-respecting lamb wears slippers, my family would say. But they weren't here and my feet sure did hurt. "I'll take the bunny slippers, please."

The clerk gave them to me. "What made you pick these?"

"Because they make me happy," I said, putting them on my tired feet.

He clapped his hands. "That's a sign telling you which way you should go. Choosing what makes you happy is the first step of the Stay True Trail!"

The clerk walked with me to the fork. I wanted to be brave but still felt afraid. "Will you come with me?"

He answered, "You have to go alone, there's only room for one. It's a rougher trail because so few lambs take the risk of being true to themselves."

I looked down at my slippers, wishing they would hop onto the first step for me.

"I'll let you in on a secret," he said with a wink.

"The secret to the Stay True trail," he whispered, "is just one step."

"Which step is that?"

"The *next* step," he said. "That's all you need to get to your dreams."

"You mean I don't have to know where the trail will take me?"

He smiled. "What would be the fun in that? There will be twists and turns, more exciting than you can imagine."

"I thought I was supposed to know where I'm trying to go?"

"Only if you want to go where you've already been," he said.

I glanced at my bunny slippers.

If my first happy heart choice made me feel this good, how much pleasure would I find on the Stay True Trail?

I took a deep breath and puffed out my chest. . . I was feeling brave.

On the first step of my new adventure, I heard nothing, nothing at all. I never knew nothing could be the scariest sound of all. “I don’t hear my heart song!” I cried to the trees, to the leaves, to the empty path ahead. Being me, the really real me, was a very hard thing to be.

Maybe I wasn’t ready. Maybe I wasn’t this brave. I turned around, ready to go back.

"Don't be afraid," the clerk called, still standing at the fork. "Hearing quiet gives you space to hear something new."

"What if you're wrong? What if I'm a lamb without a heart song?"

He smiled. "It's time to trust yourself. You cannot get lost when you follow your heart."

The sun came out and a single perfect ray lit up the next step.

I took a deep breath. "I can do this," I whispered to make myself believe. I tiptoed forward and felt primal drums inside my chest. My feet started tapping and I jumped to the next step.

On the next step I heard the soft lyrics of a sweet song, in a voice that was all my own.

Wearing bunny slippers and my new brave face, each next step got easier. I pranced and danced down the Stay True Trail to the beat of my own heart song.

On the next step, about to disappear around the bend, I found a dandelion and picked it up. I blew tiny seeds of wisdom back to the fork so others would know which way to go.

My wish for you is that when you come to your own fork, you will listen and dance to the song in your heart.

Love,

the Lamb
who was never really lost

Un • Becoming

un • be • com • ing;

The process of letting go so you can, once again, pass into a new state.

She was done being a butterfly. Over time, her wings had been torn and scars zig-zagged across her colorful mosaic body. Her dance of flight was labored now and she wondered if her song was coming to an end.

Un•become.

She flew high into the sky, far away from what she had known, looking for an answer. She nestled into the crooked branches of a tree, refusing to accept that she could only be what she had already been.

Un•become.

From her higher branch, she remembered being a caterpillar. Remembered hatching out of her egg, hungry. Molting so that her body could grow bigger and consume more. Grounding in her earth-bound body.

Un•become.

She then remembered the instinctive wisdom, a whisper inside telling her to spin into a cocoon and melt. No longer a caterpillar, but not yet a butterfly. That whisper, full of unwavering faith, promised that she had the ability to transform into something new and exquisite.

Un•become.

In the tree above the world she had once been part of, she settled into her silence. Into her stillness.

From time immortal, females have been told to become. Daughter. Student. Lover. Wife. Mother. Always becoming more.

In the quiet, she heard that message, reverberating loud and clear across tribes and generations and hearts.

Un•become.

Beneath those words, another, softer message. She leaned into the sound, until it took root and blossomed. This life, with all its identities and roles, had been its own cocoon, molded and shaped by the experience of becoming so many things.

Un•become.

The ancient feminine wisdom calmed her uncertainty and reminded her that she had an organic knowing. She braced herself on the branch, finally ready. . .

a spiritual transformation this time rather than a physical one.

Different, but the same.

Un•become.

That innate voice guided her to unravel the bindings. She unwrapped each silken thread of who she had been and laid it on the branch. She thanked each experience for its gifts and for its trials. For its hurting and for its healing.

Then she blew those threads into the wind like dandelion wishes, freeing herself from the past.

Un•become.

The scars on her wings faded, leaving a mosaic map of knowledge across her body. She breathed air into her lighter lungs and opened her heart. Now she will share the secret of un•becoming. The beauty. The wisdom. The necessity.

She will tell other tired butterflies. And the butterflies will tell the bird. And the birds will sing to all the females of the forest and the sirens of the sea.

The butterfly effect of one awakened woman will sprinkle like stardust on the wind, a whisper in our collective soul. . .

Un•becoming.

The Lovebird's Empty Nest

Life was great for the little Lovebird. She settled down in her nest with her partner and her baby lovebirds gathered around her, cuddled so close it was hard to tell where she ended and the next one began.

She taught them to love and to sing. To see the beauty in the world and to be wary of the predators.

She taught them to fly. . . forgetting that meant someday they would fly away.

One day, her nest was empty. They were all gone. So suddenly. Too soon. They promised to come back, but when they did, they felt like visitors, not nest-mates. Father Time had played a trick on her. In the blink of an eye, she went from never-enough to too-much time.

From one day craving time, to the next day, fearing time.

Her body had aged, and the feathers she had once prided herself on had fallen to the bottom of the nest. She was naked. Exposed and raw.

Embarrassed, she did the only thing she could think of. She picked up her old feathers, some gently pulled and others harshly ripped from her skin by the greedy hands of time, and started stitching together a coat. She would cover her new self with her old self.

She stitched through spring and summer.

She sewed through fall and winter.

Finally, the coat was done, a rough version of the smooth beauty she had once been. She pulled it tight around her shivering body, hoping she would feel hugged.

Instead, the awkward feather coat weighed her down.

Perhaps she had missed a stitch, or left a hole, and needed to make it tighter.

She flew to the pond to look at her reflection. But no, the pond reflected the truth. . . she saw a silly lovebird, all wrapped up in trying to be what she no longer was.

She dropped to her little bird knees. A single tear rolled down her cheek and dripped into the pond, sending ripples across the surface.

Suddenly, behind her own reflection, Mother Nature appeared, wise and kind. She wore a dress of daisies, with a crown of sunflowers woven through her long blonde hair. She stood over the Lovebird's shoulder and spoke to truth's reflection. "Why are you wearing a coat of the past?"

The Lovebird answered with a question of her own, an aching truth in her heart. "Why did you make me a Lovebird only to let time take everyone away? What good is a Lovebird with no one to love?"

Mother Nature thought for a moment, her green eyes as soft as hills of new spring grass. “Without barrenness, my darling Lovebird, there is no space for a new season.” Her words were caught on the wind, becoming butterflies dancing in the air around them. “In autumn, the leaves dry and wither, falling to the ground. The tree’s gnarled branch fingers reach into the grey sky. They are readying, you see, for winter’s snowflake kisses. They catch those kisses, then sprinkle them on the ground, blanketing the new life until spring arrives to warm the seeds into fields of waltzing wildflowers.”

The Lovebird shook her head. "I don't understand. I am not a tree or a flower or even a snowflake. I am just a lonely Lovebird who has been left behind."

"Every thing in life has a season. Every single thing grows. Evolves. Changes." Mother Nature smiled. "Even you. Even love."

The Lovebird's wings hung heavy at her side. She shook her head and a feather fell from her bulky coat.

She didn't feel changed. Or evolved.

"Because you had the courage to sit in your emptiness," Mother Nature continued, "you can transition to a new season of loving."

The little Lovebird wasn't sure that spending the last year stitching a coat out of her old feathers was brave, but who was she to argue with Mother Nature? "A new season of loving?" she asked, confused. "But I am alone now. Who will I love?"

"Turn your love inward. Love yourself." Mother Nature gently tugged on the coat of feathers. "After all, who can love you better than you?"

The Lovebird looked at her reflection and frowned. "How can I love me? I am sad and ugly, hiding in a silly old coat."

"You were never ugly," Mother Nature said, bending down and smoothing the ripples in the pond. "Look again."

The Lovebird let the coat fall off her shoulders. She leaned over the water, until she could see every inch of herself. No longer naked and sad, but. . . changing. What was that on her shoulder? On her chin? On her belly?

Tiny buds. Downy feathers. New beginnings.

"I've been so afraid of being alone," she whispered. "Of not being needed. Or wanted."

"You are not abandoned," Mother Nature said softly, "unless you abandon yourself."

The Lovebird caressed her new feathers. They were different from the feathers of her youth. Deeper and richer, they filled her with hope.

"This new season," Mother Nature promised, "*this* is the best season of all."

The Lovebird was still trying to adjust to her new feathers, and her new thoughts. "How? Why? What do I do now?"

Mother Nature smiled and the sun shone brighter. "You *love* with every fiber of your being. Accept that you are love, that your body is love, that your being is love, and then a wondrous thing happens." Her face glowed and the air sparkled like radiant diamonds. "You will be *in* love all the time!"

Mother Nature gave her a gentle nudge toward the water. The Lovebird took a deep breath and dove into the warm, deep pond, letting the water and the wisdom wash over her. Through her.

When she emerged from the water, Mother Nature was gone, but that was okay. She now understood that alone didn't mean lonely. She had the trees that loved her and cradled her nest every night. She had the song of faraway birds that filled the quiet air.

And most important of all, she had herself.

The Lovebird chose the best feathers from the coat and lined her nest with the warmth of their memories. She surrendered to the seasons of love and went from lonely to loving beyond her wildest imagination.

Inflated with love, she soared through the sky, singing the song of the lovebird for all to hear. . .

Remember that you *are* love, and you can be *in* love all the time!

Re • Uniting

re • u • nit • ing

The process of coming together again after a period of separation or disunity.

Inside of me, I have lungs and a heart. Blood and bones.

But there is also a yearning. An ache. A chasm that has split me down the middle.

No one can see the galaxy of lonely stars floating around inside my human body but the emptiness is heavier than the bones of twenty generations.

Then I read a book and one line pierces my heart. I feel like it was written just for me.

I am a spiritual being having a human experience.

Those words help me understand that I am lonely. . . for myself. For my better half. For my higher self.

Those words explain the fracture that cuts through the middle of my being like the Thanksgiving wishbone that gets ripped apart.

Somehow in my own separation, I've pulled the smaller half.

I feel trapped, weighted in the limitations of my physical body.

I have spent my life searching for my higher self. As I've gotten older, the barrier that separates us has thinned. Now it is only a layer of onion skin, paper-thin and translucent.

Desperate to reach her, I stand on my tippy toes until my legs ache, stretching my fingertips toward her, so close to touching it hurts. I collapse back into the cavern of my body, hoping the winds of time will shift the barrier so I can get a better grip.

In the dark penance of night, I am afraid I am not good enough for her.

I am less. She is more.

I am frantic. She is calm.

I am unworthy. She is invaluable.

I long to feel whole. For the emptiness to be filled.

I desire her with every fiber of my being.

One day, a random day indeed, she peeks over the edge of the onion skin veil and says one word. “Gravity.”

So simple. So obvious. Gravity reveals it would be easier for her to come down here than it is for me to get up there.

All this time it never, ever occurred to me that my spiritual self was longing to sink into my human self. “So why haven’t you come down to me?” I ask.

"I've been trying," she says. "For years and years, I have been poking holes into the onion skin that separates us. Shining the light of love on you."

"Sometimes I have felt close to you and for brief seconds, all was right with my soul." I sigh and my shoulders serpentine down my back. "But the more I feel you, the more I miss you."

"I've been trying to come down to you," she whispers on the wind, "as much as you've been trying to reunite with me."

I hold my breath. Is that possible?

She smiles. "You don't have to worry. We will be reunited. The only question is, will it be in this realm?"

"What realm?" I ask.

"The body you are in, the one we chose together, light years ago."

“There is a door,” she says.

I look closer, and in the veins of the onion skin, I see the curves of an old arched door. I jump up, reaching for her. Always reaching for her. “Come through!” I cry.

“It’s locked. And you have the key.”

I reach in my pockets, even though I know there is nothing there. “You should have the key! You’re the better half.”

"I am not better," she says. "I am simply love."

Feeling small, my spine bows like a crescent moon. I have been trying to get better at loving all my life. Inhale love. Exhale love. I try and I try, but I keep losing my breath.

She reaches down and lifts my chin. "I might be pure love but you, my darling, were brave enough to plant yourself in the nitty grittiness of life. You had the courage to transition into imperfection Into scared and scarred." She smiles. "You are the beautiful flaws. The baby steps. You are the falling down and getting back up again. And if you'll let me, I want to experience this adventure with you."

"That's all I want, too!" I cry.

"Because I am simply love," she cautions, "you have to allow me to love it all."

I grin. This is all I've ever wanted.

"I want to love your husband. The one you and I chose together."

"I want to love him more, too," I say quickly.

"I want to love him for giving you so much freedom."

I think for a minute and say carefully, "Well, yes I adore the freedom. . . but sometimes that freedom feels like too much space. You will fix that, right?"

"I can't fix. I can only love. I will love the freedom. And the space. I will even love your fear."

I don't see the point in that. I want her to make it better.

"You must love what is all around you," she says. "Even the young man who is breaking your daughter's heart. He has shown her what love can be, even if he can't show her anymore."

"Wait a minute," I say. "How can you love someone who is hurting my daughter?"

"I am not asking you to be pure love, like I am. I am asking you to let me experience life beside you. Within you. I am asking if you can let me love it all. Can you be that open? That is the key that will open this door."

"I can try," I say, feeling defeated. "I have been trying for a long time."

"You don't have to do it alone," she promises. "The more you let me in, the more I can love everything for you. For us. You will ground me, and I will help you fly."

"Tell me how," I whisper.

"The first step," she answers, "is accepting that love is the question and the answer. The beginning and the end."

She settles into me, into that space, and I feel her love.

It's time to be at peace. . . and not in pieces.

I close my eyes and breathe in a slow, deep breath. I infuse the air with love and let it fill my lungs. Slowly, trust replaces the ache. Faith fills the chasm.

A spiritual being having a human experience.

A human being having a spiritual experience.

Reuniting.

About the Author

Deborah Monk uses story and art to empower women and girls to find their voice.

Books are portals to other worlds. When I finish a book and it touched my heart, I've always wished there was a talisman or a keepsake I could take with me back into the real world, a physical reminder of the message of the story.

I designed this necklace and bracelet so I could keep the meaning of the stories close to me. You can find them at:

DeborahMonkBooks.etsy.com

dig deep
fly high
dig deep
fly high

I have made each of these stories into a handmade book. The book covers are printed on seed paper that, if planted, will sprout snapdragons, poppies, and eight other wildflowers. The pages are printed on handmade paper harvested from the Lokta bush that grows high atop the sun-kissed Himalayan Mountains.

Email me at deb@deborahmonk.com and tell me your favorite story and I will send you a 20% coupon for:

DeborahMonkBooks.etsy.com

Wings and a Tail: Part of growing up meant giving up her angel wings and mermaid tail . . . will she be able to reclaim her magic?

The Dancing Acorn: An acorn settles down and grows into a big oak tree, eventually feeling like a spectator of life. Then Mother Nature asks the question, "Who do you want to be?"

The Lost Lamb: After following the herd down the well-worn path, will this little lamb find her courage to follow her heart and find her own path?

Un•becoming: Tired of being a butterfly, she flies high into a tree and settles into stillness. Can she find the strength to transform once again?

The Lovebird's Empty Nest: Alone in her empty nest, will this little lovebird find the answer to the question in her heart. . .Who can I love now that I'm all alone?

Re•uniting: Feeling fractured, can a woman find a way to re-connect with her higher self?

Made in the USA
Middletown, DE
05 October 2023